CRINKLED PAGES OF MEMORIES

AMARTTAN ROY CHOWDHURY

Copyright © Amarttan Roy Chowdhury
All Rights Reserved.

This book has been published with all efforts taken to make the material error-free after the consent of the author. However, the author and the publisher do not assume and hereby disclaim any liability to any party for any loss, damage, or disruption caused by errors or omissions, whether such errors or omissions result from negligence, accident, or any other cause.

While every effort has been made to avoid any mistake or omission, this publication is being sold on the condition and understanding that neither the author nor the publishers or printers would be liable in any manner to any person by reason of any mistake or omission in this publication or for any action taken or omitted to be taken or advice rendered or accepted on the basis of this work. For any defect in printing or binding the publishers will be liable only to replace the defective copy by another copy of this work then available.

To my parents, who didn't know that I was writing a book but still supported me somehow......

Contents

Foreword

All the stories and characters in this book are fictional. I discovered them while turning pages of boring classes in school. But now I feel that my classroom and the window beside my table helped me discovering the not-so-good author inside me. Mistakes are obvious. This book is packed with crime, mystery, love, sorrow and radiating happiness within all ugly components of the world. I hope everyone will like it!

Preface

We all are captured somewhere around the world with full of obligations which denies our wish to dream. No one except the person itself can help to achieve the dreams but this book will try to take the reader to another world for some hours to experience the fream world of crime, love and much more!

ACKNOWLEDGEMENTS

I am very grateful to all my friends and the supporters on social media who encouraged me to write this book. Also I would like to thank all those people who tried discouraging me because those bitter experiences helped me today express my words and I feel that those discouraging people would be proud of me.

I would also thanks **Google** and the travel vloggers on **Youtube** to help me get familiar with various beautiful places around the world during lockdown!

ACKNOWLEDGMENTS

[illegible]

PROLOGUE

Writers are just a bunch of overthinkers who note down their thoughts.

Contents

I

A Painter's Tragedy

"Hey Chloe, get down here, I want to talk to you right now"!

Chloe hurried down the stairs to the living room where her mother was standing in front of the fireplace pointing at a framed picture on the mantle.

"Why did you put that there"?

"I didn't", Chloe responded taken aback by her mother's overly aggressive gesturing.

"Um, I think you did because you are the only other person in this house and I didn't put it there so it had to be you".

"No, it wasn't me and I have no idea what that picture is about so why would I put it there"?

The framed painting was of an old house with an elderly couple and a small child standing in front. In the distance was a wheat field and farther away a snow-capped mountain that towered over the valley. In the corner of the painting was a faded signature and date, **TJ Stand, 1733**.

Chloe wondered who TJ Stand was and how they ended up with a painting by him. She took the frame down and set it in a box on the floor that she would take to the donation centre later in the day.

"Hey mom, who was TJ Stand"?

"I have no idea and frankly I don't care. I need to start planting the rose bushes so while I do that you get rid of the picture and put the one that was there back".

"Put it back, I don't know where it is".

"It's probably where you stashed it when you put that one up". Her mother stormed off in the direction of the kitchen and Chloe could hear her gathering together the tools she would need to pot this season's rose bushes.

"I told you, I didn't put that painting up there so I have no idea where the other one is" she said to herself. This was getting to be aggravating since she really didn't like being called a liar. She turned and hurried up the stairs to the attic where she would look first. When Chloe opened the door and flipped the light switch she saw it, there in the corner leaning up against the Christmas decoration boxes stacked in the corner. She grabbed it and took it back to the living room and placed it on the mantle. It was a framed painting of a blue whale breaching the water. It was a beautiful picture but not one that held any sentimental value.

"Mom, I found the picture and put it on the mantle. I'm going into town to drop this box off at the donation center; is there anything you need while I'm out"?

"No, but hurry back because I'm going to need your help", the back screen door slammed shut behind Chloe's mom.

The drive into town was uneventful and when Chloe pulled into the parking lot of the donation center she parked the truck, grabbed the box from the back and headed inside. She walked straight to the back of the store where donations were left and rang the bell at the desk.

"Can I help you", the lady asked?

"Yes, I want to donate these items and wondered where I should put them".

"Just leave them right there, I'll get to them later today. Do you need a receipt"?

"No, that's fine, thank you".

"You're welcome, have a blessed day", she spun around a returned to the back of the store where she busied herself unpacking other donated items.

Chloe took note of the box and the picture inside and decided to check on the painter over the weekend. Right now, she needed to return home and get busy on the rose bushes. When she pulled into the driveway she immediately went to the garden where her mother was planting and set about doing the business of gardening. For some reason the dirt smelled old and musty not the usual fertilizer odour she was used to but she put it out of her mind and started making furrows for the roses.

Chloe woke with a start and noticed the time, it was 3:00 AM, she'd been startled by a loud noise coming from downstairs. She got up and put on her robe and headed in the direction of the sound. When she stepped into the living room and flipped on the light switch, she saw it, the painting was on the mantle again the same painting she had left in town.

"What the hell is going on" she whispered to herself, "that can't be there". She rubbed her eyes, turned off the light and waited for a few seconds. When she turned the lights back on the painting was still there. Chloe immediately ran up the stairs to the attic and opened the door, again the whale painting was leaning up against the

Christmas decoration boxes stacked in the corner. She was aghast and grabbed the painting and rushed back downstairs to replace the painting on the mantle, if her mother saw it she would be furious. Taking the painting to her room she found a blanket and wrapped it up to take it to the donation center first thing. She'd get up early and head to town before her mother ever realized what was going on. Before heading back to bed, she pinched herself to make sure she wasn't dreaming, she wasn't and her arm hurt, she was awake.

At 6:30 Chloe got up and dressed quickly and headed downstairs carrying the wrapped painting under here arm. She grabbed the keys, heard her mother stirring in the kitchen and hollered out,

"Mom, I need to get to town I forgot something yesterday. Can I get you anything while I'm there"?

"No, thanks for asking though, see ya when you get back. Be safe, love ya"!

"I'm going to stop at the Library so I'll be a couple hours".

"OK sweetie, see you later".

Chloe stopped at the espresso stand and ordered a large coffee and decided to hit the library first. She wanted to look into TJ Stand first before she donated the painting again.

The library was relatively small but had a good research area so she headed there first. Stopping at the desk she asked the librarian where she should look for information about TJ Stand and saw the smile that crossed the librarians face. She lit up and told Chloe a story she'd never heard before.

"Well, TJ Stand was the original founder of our little valley in the early 1700's. He was a painter from England that came here to make his fortune but was never successful at that so he decided to settle this area first. He called this township Snowden in honour of the mountain that claimed his beloved son when they came here. His wife and daughter survived the trip across the mountain but his son fell into a chasm and was never found. It was a tragedy of unimaginable grief, one TJ never fully recovered from. The few paintings he completed were sold off for pennies and after 3 short years the family disappeared and were never heard from again. Nobody knows what happened but some suspect they were killed to make way for immigrants from Ireland. The town's name was changed to Centerville, and it grew up from there. The saying is that there is one painting which was never found and is worth hundreds of thousands of dollars because it has clues to what happened to TJ and his family. I don't know if it's true but wow, how awesome would that be".

"Do you have any idea what the painting was"?

"Sure, it was of him and his family standing in front of their home. The house is gone now but the place that was built in its place is a nursery where beautiful rose bushes are sold, I have our gardener buy there every couple of years. The yellow roses are so sweet smelling and absolutely stunning".

Chloe was in shock they had built their house on the very property TJ Stand had owned.

"Do you have any pictures of the painting; I'd love to see it"?

"As a matter of fact, I do. I'll just go get the book written about this man. It is a good read".

The librarian returned with an open book and showed her the picture of the painting. It was the same, it was the one in the truck.

"I'd like to check this out if it's OK"?

“Sure, when you’re ready to leave stop at the desk and I’ll have it ready to go. Can I have your library card”?

Chloe gave over her card, took a deep breath and headed for the front desk, questions were stuck in here head. Why was the painting in her house, how did it get there and what happened to the Stand’s?

When Chloe got home, she took the painting into the house and placed it on the mantle alongside the painting of the whale. With the book she’d just checked out from the library in hand she went to the garden where her mother was already working at mixing fertilizer. Chloe placed the open book on the table and called her mother over and started telling her story.

“First of all, you are not going to believe what I’m about to tell you but it’s the truth. Yesterday you told me to get rid of a painting you thought I had placed on the mantle, but mom I didn’t and took it to the donation center and left it there. Early this morning I was startled awake and went to find out what had wakened me and found the painting I had returned on the mantle the whale picture was once again upstairs in the attic. I decided to find out about the painting because there was no reason for it to be on the mantle. Something weird was happening so I decided to stop at the library and ask some questions.

It turns out the painter, TJ Stand, was the original founder of this little town and he named it Snowden in honour of his son that was killed when they made their way to this place in the early 1700’s. The grief was too much for them and the entire family disappeared after 3 years. All of the paintings were sold off except one, the one we have. How we ended up with it I don’t have a clue but we do have it and it’s worth a lot of money. According to the librarian it will tell us what happened to the family”.

"This is a joke, right"?

"No mom, it is not and I kept the painting, it's on the mantle. I think we should check it out maybe solve a mystery and get rich at the same time".

"OK, let's get these plants potted and check out your theory".

By the time they finished with the rose bushes it was late afternoon and they were hungry. Dinner consisted of snack food since neither of them wanted to waste any time looking into this mystery.

"Chloe, grab two magnifying glasses and we'll pour over this painting to see what is hidden".

"I don't even know what to look for, the librarian didn't give any hint as to what might be obscured from view she did say they 'disappeared' so she thought they could have been murdered, but how would he have known so I'm thinking not".

As Chloe and her mother scanned the painting they noticed something odd, a well was obscured at the back of the property hidden under a bush.

"Look at that, it's a hidden well, let's go check it out".

Together they gathered tools to uncover the well and find its opening. After clearing the debris they found what they thought was a well but was instead a shallow grave and inside were three bodies, two of them were wrapped in sheets and the third was laying across the top of them, there appeared to be a hole in the side of his head. When the coroner had finished his examination, it was determined that TJ Stand had killed his wife and child out of grief and then himself. Time had hidden their bodies but they would now would be buried in the town's cemetery. Apparently, the ghost of TJ was so distraught with what he had done he was determined to make find a way to get someone to look for himself and his family and lay them to rest.

The painting was sold to the town for $1.00 and hung in the library. The story of TJ Stand and his family was written in the town's history ledger so that people would never forget the sorrow of the loss that led to such a tragedy.

II

Father

"I wish to meet Mr. Pradip Sengupta," the girl told the security man at the gate.

"Who?" the security man asked rather rudely. Perhaps he was annoyed to see a young girl at the factory gate early in the morning distracting his men's attention at a time when workers were queuing at the punching area for going out after the night shift.

"Mr Pradip Sengupta, Chemical engineer," the girl repeated slowly, stressing each syllable.

"Sorry, no such person is working here!" The security man did not think twice to answer her.

The girl appeared uncertain and remained at the gate for some more time.

"Didn't I make myself clear? There is no one by that name working here. So don't stand there blocking the way," he said annoyed, summarily dismissing her.

The girl stepped out and started to return disappointed when she saw an elderly man coming to the factory.

"Excuse me, sir, can you tell me where Mr. Pradip Sengupta is working now? I heard he was employed here earlier."

"Mr. Pradip Sengupta? I'm sorry, my dear child, you'll not find Mr. Sengupta here."

"Oh," her face fell. "Is he dead?"

"No, he is very much alive."

"Then do you know where he is now?"

"I said you will not find him here, because he is now working in our head office."

The girl let out a small sigh. "But the security man said Mr. Sengupta doesn't work in this company."

"The security men are outsourced people. They keep changing. They know only those officers who are working here presently," he explained.

"I see." The girl seemed a little relieved to know that Mr. Sengupta was still in the company.

"I would like to meet him, but I cannot go that far. Wouldn't he come here at all?" she asked hopefully.

"He might visit here once or twice a year. Contact our office and they will tell you when he is expected next," he advised and started walking towards the factory gate.

"Thank you, sir," she called out but in the dim of the company's siren that went off suddenly to announce the shift change drowned her expression of gratitude.

"You seemed very happy, Selina. Did you meet Mr. Sengupta?" her mother Jennifer asked as soon as the girl reached home.

"No mummy, he no longer works there," she answered.

"Oh! That's unfortunate," Jennifer commented. "I was hoping that you may be able to meet him."

Selina let out a small laugh. "I didn't say mummy that he had resigned and gone. He is very much in the service but works in their head office."

"Oh. It's as good as he has left the company. I don't, therefore, understand why you look euphoric that he is now inaccessible."

"You know what he is now?", Selina asked.

"How do I know? I've no news of him for the last eighteen years."

"He has gone up many career rungs and is now the Vice President (Operations). Isn't it wonderful?"

"A distant moon is no use when you are looking for light in the darkness," her mother remarked. "He has become a Vice President in the company doesn't surprise me. I knew that he would take advantage of every opportunity that comes his way, would seek out every angle to maximize his abilities and strive hard to improve his job skills for advancing his career. But many men as they climb up the ladder of success become haughtier and self-centered. So don't be very sure that he would agree to help you."

"Oh, mummy, don't be pessimistic. If my name means 'a star in the sky', meeting the moon poses no difficulty. I was told that Mr Sengupta comes to this city once or twice a year, and fortunately, he is coming next week for a conference. I've already taken an appointment to meet him when he comes. Let's keep our fingers crossed." Selina said.

Selina felt rather nervous as she waited at the reception lounge for the appointment. Except for the low buzzing of the air conditioner, there was perfect silence in the office, occasionally broken by the insistence ringing of the telephones. There were few trade magazines and newspapers on the wooden center table in front of her but she was not in a good frame of mind to flip through them to while away the time. She was asked to come at 2.00 p.m. and it was already 1.55 p.m. As time ticked by, her apprehension multiplied. She saw many young and elderly persons returning after lunch, but her imagination of how Mr. Sengupta would look like failed to match with any of them. After what seemed an eternity, she found an athletic-looking man getting down from a chauffeur driven car and going up the stairs followed by few other persons. "This cannot be him; this man looks too young to be Mr. Sengupta," she mused. A few minutes later, the lady receptionist called her. "Ms. Selina, Mr. Sengupta would see you now. Come with me, and I'll show you the room."

The girl followed her.

"Come in, Ms. Selina," a *strident voice greeted* as soon as she knocked on the massive door of the conference room. The person she thought could not be Mr. Sengupta was sitting behind a long glass top table. There were many chairs around it. "Come and take your seat," he invited authoritatively pointing a chair near him.

After she was seated comfortably, he asked, "Now, Ms. Selina, you said you wanted to discuss with me something very personal. What's it? Make it very short. No long stories. I can allot only five minutes for you since I've some more engagements to attend before I return by the evening flight," he cautioned as an introduction.

"Well," she began hesitatingly. "My name is Selina Sengupta," she began.

"I know. The receptionist told me. Very odd name, I'd say," he commented, interrupting her.

She ignored it and said, "I was asked to meet you by one Jennifer Samuel. Hope you still remember her?" she asked.

"Jennifer! You mean to say Jenny Samuel of 49 Ripon Street?" he asked, suspiciously.

"Yes, Jenny Samuel. She was also known by the name Jennifer Sengupta. I happened to be her only daughter!"

"You are.... You're my daughter? My God!" he exclaimed, stunned at her revelation.

For some time, he just gaped at her without speaking. "I'm sorry my dear child; I should have recognized you the moment you came in. You've got the same features as Jenny. I'm sorry," he apologized again. "How's Jenny? Is she all right?"

"She's now all right. She had open-heart surgery after she had a near-fatal attack about two years ago, and now she's on rest. Whatever savings she had evaporated with that one ailment and since she had to resign her job at the Loreto Day School for Girls, she now finds it hard to support my further education. Incidentally, I got the 67th rank in the medical entrance exam but we have no wherewithal to proceed further. That's when she advised me to meet you and request you whether you can help me," she said without any ill feeling. Suddenly, as if remembering something, she looked at her watch to know how much more time she had from the allotted five minutes.

"Don't bother about the time," he chastised her. Then he picked up the intercom and instructed someone, "Reschedule my return flight to tomorrow morning and fix my afternoon meeting at 4 O'clock. Ok?" He did not say the reason for change of plans. Turning to her he said, "Now we've all the time in the world for you to fill up the past eighteen years of emptiness," he said beaming.

Selina was elated to know that he had acknowledged her as his daughter. He had told her not to make long stories, but as she filled the long years of vacuum, it changed from stories to novellas and novellas to novel but he listened to her attentively, sometimes appearing pensive and sometimes amused at her anecdotes.

"I missed the thrill of seeing you growing up," he said sadly. As if remembering something, he asked, "How's Bob Samuel? It's been long time since I saw him."

"I'm sorry, grandpa expired about six years ago. He died in his sleep. A silent attack," she said succinctly.

"Oh! I'm sorry, no one informed me," he lamented, "otherwise I would've attended the funeral." He was silent for some time. Then he added, "Bob uncle was a wonderful person, and a perfect gentleman. Though he was working in a cinema theatre, everyone in the locality, from the street cobblers, rickshaw pullers, doctors, engineers and others respected him. I've not seen such a lovable person anywhere in my long career. He was a good counsellor too and had the ability to make the person realize where he or she erred and correct themselves. People would openly discuss their problems. He was a good listener and an empathetic guide. His nephew was my classmate in the college and he introduced me to Bob Uncle. Bob uncle used to give us complimentary passes for English movies and for Film festivals. He was very fond of me."

"Then why didn't you try to meet him after you broke up the relationship?" Selina questioned, almost accusing him.

Sengupta did not reply immediately. Then appearing somewhat maudlin he said, "I was ashamed to meet him. I had failed in his expectations. Jenny had returned to her father's house within one year of marriage. That would have given their neighbors good subject for gossiping. I thought Bob uncle would counsel his daughter and send her back, but somehow he failed to convince her. I was also afraid Jenny might shut the door on my face if I go there. That was one of my greatest miscalculations," he admitted. "I have heard people say that Jenny left our house because of frequent mother-in-law - daughter-in-law squabbles but that was not true." He was silent for some time. Perhaps he did not wish to discuss the matter.

"Ha," he said suddenly. "I forgot to congratulate you for getting the 67th rank. Not a small achievement. Don't worry about college fees and other expenses. Leave it to me." He took out his checkbook and began to write. Then he paused and asked, "What name shall I put on the check?"

"You may write it out to Jennifer Sengupta," Selina replied. "She never reverted it to her original name."

He appeared as if someone slapped him. Then recovering fast, he completed the name. "I've made it out for one hundred thousand rupees. I guess it would cover the initial expenses. Here's my card," he said fishing out a card from his wallet. "You can call me anytime for anything you need. Now, let's meet my colleagues here. I wish to introduce my daughter to them," he said getting up.

As he introduced her to few of his colleagues, he said, "Okay my child, it was a wonderful time speaking to you. I would like to hear from you more when we meet next. Now I've a meeting at 4 O'clock."

"Ok, papa, then 'bye."

"How would go back?" he asked.

"As usual, by bus. Why?"

"No, I'll ask the driver to drop you at your house," he offered.

She was sorry that she could not remain with him for some more time.

"Don't look gloomy, my child," he said. "I'll come next month on a short vacation. Needs to meet my folks here and would like to come to your house, if your mother does not object," he said.

"She'll not; I guarantee. You're always welcome."

"Then we'll meet next month."

As she was walking through the narrow lane towards her house after she got down from the car at Ripon Street, she wondered whether it was a daydream or actually happened. Everything seemed so unreal and hazy. She had finally met her dad. Now she could tell her irksome neighbours and friends that she was not an illegitimate child as some of them doubted.

As soon as the door opened, Jenny asked, "Could you meet him, Selina?"

"Of course! But mummy, the questions I had mentally prepared to ask him while waiting to see him, eclipsed when the moon appeared. Yet I'm happy that dad has given two long hours of his busy time to know each other. In fact, I remember reading somewhere that lunar eclipse is a time to look inwardly to find out our defects and get rid of those patterns. I think it is high time that you self-reflect your life and accept that you've grossly failed to understand your husband."

Jenny did not make any comment.

Exactly one month later, Selina went to the company's New Alipore guesthouse to meet her father. This time, she was more relaxed and did not have her earlier nervousness of meeting a stranger.

Selina had some questions numbered chronologically to ask him, but when he came embracing her with open arms, they just evaporated and all she could ask him about his job and his life in Gurgaon. He replied to her questions in one or two simple words, but did not elaborate. She was not sure whether he had remarried and or not after the estrangement. It seemed awkward to open that subject.

Suddenly he asked, "Did your mother tell you the reason for our break-up?"

"No. Mummy doesn't like to talk about it. She always appeared irritated when I questioned her. If the reason is not embarrassing, can you enlighten me?" Selina asked becoming a little bold.

He laughed lightly and said, "There was no embarrassing situation in it, but let me summarized it and say that it was entirely my mistake. In my younger days, I considered my job as the most important thing than anything else. I was working in shifts in those days and on many time I could come home after Jenny was in deep slumber or after she had left for school. She suffered my lack of attention demurely, and never complained, and I thought she encouraged my attempt to augment our income by working overtime. On that fateful day, which was our first marriage anniversary, I had taken a leave and promised to take her to a popular Hindi cinema and later to a sumptuous dinner at an expensive hotel, but on the previous evening two of our shift engineers failed to turn up and I had to do three shifts at a stretch. When I reached home in the morning, I was a dead duck and slept throughout the day forgetting about the promise and the outing. Jenny could not contain her disappointment and all her suppressed emotions burst out and she hit the ceiling crying that I loved my work more than her. I did not reason with her about not keeping my word. I thought she was a sensible woman and knew my work profile. At that time, I did not know she was pregnant. Jenny had told me that she would tell me a happy news on our wedding day, but that night she behaved like a trussed bird. The next day she packed up her things and left without even telling a goodbye to me or to my mother. That was the last time we saw her. My mother was very much distressed and had often counselled me to bring Jenny back. But my ego persuaded me against it and I thought she had walked out from my house without any reason, and she should come back if she really loved me. Unfortunately, without our knowing, days turned to weeks, and weeks to months, months to years, and when my mother died two years later, I found myself alone. It was then I opted for a transfer." He was silent for a long moment.

Selina wanted to comfort her father, but she did not know how he would react to her sudden expression of love.

"I'm sorry, papa. I thought you are a villain to desert my poor mummy."

"You're perfectly right, my dear child," he said. "I know how difficult to bring up a child alone all these years. I realize now that in a marriage there was no defeat or win. No partner would gain or lose anything by compromising. One thing I would like to caution you. After you become a doctor, remember that profession may be important, but family is more valuable. Balance your work and family. That is one lesson, I learnt from my life," he said almost apologetically.

For long time they remained silent.

"Come, let us go to Quest Malls or Acropolis Mall or any other good malls here and buy some dresses for you. You may need some good clothes when you go the medical college. Afterwards, we'll have lunch in their food court. Ok?" he offered.

"Ok. I'm excited." She was thrilled at the prospect of shopping at these expensive malls. In her shoestring budget, shopping at malls was a distant dream.

She was surprised when he directed the driver to go to Ripon Street. "Let's go to your house first. Wouldn't it be wonderful if your mummy joins us?"

III

Endless

What a sad, miserable environment today! It seems that all the sorrows and grief of the world have swallowed up this old age home. In this old age home live the elderly parents who have been taken care of by the modern children. The young men and women are educated only in a way of biblical lore. Their humanity is like that of a wild animal. Not even a wild animal maybe, because we can see animals protecting and helping each other in survival.

Nirmal is one of the favorite members of this endless old age home. Nirmal Chatterjee has died. Everyone has been quite as dead since morning. His wife was sitting quietly on the bed looking at the pictures from the old album. Both Nirmal and his wife Suchitra worked in a government school. They were one of the most kind and charitable couple of their time. They both taught in school for more than forty years! Their son Ravi was a brilliant student and got scholarship in Chicago University for studying Literature. He is a professor now in United States.

Ravi has not visited his parents for about 9 years. Nirmal and Suchitra were very alone. So they often went to the orphanage and spent time with the small children. They taught the children for free, gave the children clothes during occasions and also Suchitra cooked food for them every Sunday and they all sat and ate together. But these days probably ended today. Because Nirmal was no more.

Nirmal Babu's health was very bad in the last few months. His condition kept deteriorating. Although his son and son's wife was informed, they didn't even bother to visit their father and help in his treatment. Since Nirmal was sick and Suchitra herself was quite aged to take care, they decided to send Nirmal and Suchitra to this old age home named **'Endless'**. Maybe the name signifies the *endless sorrow the members of this old age home face throughout their life.* Ravi gave excuses that they were too busy in work and tried to convince everyone that life in USA is more hard and tiresome than India and promised to send money to Nirmal's doctor for his treatment.

Disha entered Nirmal Babu's room when Nirmal Babu's wife Suchitra was staring at the pictures quietly with moist eyes. Her eyes reflected sorrow and hate. Disha's life was quite similar to other happy members of this old age home. Her daughter refused to take responsibility, and then husband died. Her son was a drunkard and obviously not in condition to take care of her. So her daughter decided to send her to this old age home.

Disha: Didi, you must eat something or else you will fall sick. Ypu didn't ate anything since yesterday. Don't keep the pain inside. No one's birth or death is in our hands. I brought some Muri (Puffed rice) for you. Please eat this.

Suchitra: I was ready for this day Disha. Doctor had already said that he hardly had 3 months to live. But he was very brave, he lived for 5 months more. My only regret is that the man for whom he spent his whole life, Ravi, did not come today. When he got the news of his father's departure, he said that if I needed any money, then I should tell him.

Suchitra's eyes began to water.

Disha: Don't cry Didi, I feel very bad when you cry.

Disha tried to give consolation to Suchitra but she could hardly control her tears.

Suchitra: Ravi lives in a distant country. But nowadays it takes a couple of hours to get here from there. Couldn't come? Tell me!

Nirmal obeyed all his wishes, even though he didn't have much money, when Ravi insisted on buying that expensive laptop, his father borrowed money from all over and bought it. Nirmal never bought anything for himself. But he always fulfilled Ravi's demands.

Disha: Didi, Ravi is your son, look how successful he is working outside today!

Tears rolled down over Suchitra's cheek and she said in a broken voice, "That's why Ravi sold his mother and father."

Disha's eyes were full of water. She wanted to say something but for a strange pain in her, everything got stuck in her throat.

Suchitra: I remember a poem today,

'I know only you are, so I am
You are alive so I live
The more I get, the more I check on you
You don't know as much as I know.'

Disha: I'm bringing tea, you haven't ate anything since morning.

Suchitra sat on the bed looking outside the window. The sky was clear and she could see the path far way endlessly expanding like the human life between birth and death. When Disha was going out of the room, she saw a young man of thirty-five years standing by the door. Head bowed in shame. Even though he wore expensive clothes, his shame and suffering have erased all the prices. Probably he was listening to everything the two old women were saying.

Disha said, "Didi"

Suchitra turned around to look what happened and she was startled at the sight and said,"Ravi!"

IV

Deaf And Dumb

Just another week. Started off the same as every other week. A sharp monotone beep at 8:25 scattered the reluctant cliques, and the students slumped away to their first period. Once a squad of talkative girls cleared out from in front of her locker, she flung the door open, replaced the headphones in her pocket with a handful of honey candies, heaved a mountain of books for the morning classes into her arms, and kicked the door shut again. As most days, this gave her about two minutes to get halfway across school to get to her first class. She bustled through the halls, keeping her head down and weaving through the crowds of fellow stragglers.

She emerged through the doorway just as the second bell of the day finished ringing. As she took her usual seat in the back left corner of the room, her teacher, Mrs. Aniston-Bell, arose from her desk and walked to the front of the class. These first five minutes or so of class were the morning announcements, never really important, so it gave her a chance to dig around for the right notebook and get out her needlessly-massive geography textbook. She also liked to use this time to sing out the song that's been stuck in her head all morning.

She discovered some 90s pop songs this week. She was humming one of those songs, "You are my fire/ my desire/ believe....."

Mrs. Aniston-Bell was a likeable teacher. She had this quirky energy about her that somehow made geography fun. Also, she had pretty hair: dirty blonde and as long as her last name. She felt little guilty not paying attention to mam's announcements, but she was nearing the bridge now. She couldn't stop her performance now. She could hear parts of what Mrs. Aniston-Bell was saying anyway: kids' birthdays for the week, grilled cheese for lunch, someone set the boys' bathroom on fire. It's the same headlines every week.

"...and I want everyone to try to make him feel welcome. So just to take a minute sometime today to say hello... Adrianna, could you stop singing, please?" Suddenly, everyone had turned around in their desk and was staring at her. Adrianna sank into her desk, reluctantly rotating a fist over her chest as she looked up at her disgruntled teacher.

It was then that she noticed the boy next to Mrs. Aniston-Bell, making his way to an empty desk in the front row. He had short, brown hair that was slicked over to the left. He was quite tall. And he was wearing sunglasses. How come he got to wear sunglasses inside? Also, he was carrying some kind of stick. Was he a ninja? Some type of superhero? A deranged *UPS* man?

Ahh...She had been reading too much of science-fiction and stuff which is having its effect now.

Either way, Adrianna knew she had to meet this boy in sunglasses.

The rest of the morning continued without a sign of the boy in sunglasses. Lunch was indeed grilled cheese. Adrianna always got her lunch from the cafeteria in a to-go box so she could eat on a bench outside. Most days she just brought her own lunch, mainly to avoid the prison-like setting that is the cafeteria, but she couldn't say no to a grilled cheese.

After lunch was study hall with Mr. S. Nobody really knew what the 'S' stood for. Most of the boys in school just called him "Coach". Study hall with Mr. S was great. She could listen to her music the whole hour, giving her a chance to focus and get done all of the homework that she "forgot" to do last night. Huhh! What a great reason. Every one of us give or gave this excuse. Every one of us either say that we were out of station for some work or we sacrifice the life of our relatives in our leave applications in school.

Even if he didn't like people listening to music in his classroom, Mr. S would never notice. He usually spent the entire hour staring at his computer, watching recordings of last Friday's varsity football game.

Today, Adrianna was particularly focused with the help of the hits on her playlists. She began to inadvertently tap her pencil against the desk to the beat of each song as she worked. Becoming so absorbed, a sudden voice from behind her nearly made her jump out of her seat. "Is that *Toto*?" She tried to swing herself around in the least awkward way that she could manage. It was the boy in sunglasses.

"I'd recognize that beat anywhere," he continued. A smirk appeared on his face as he started to bang his hands on the desk, mimicking the beat of the song. He was much cuter up close. Unfortunately, his smile didn't stay too long. He ceased banging the desk, as his face started growing pink. He cleared his throat and dropped his head. Must have thought she didn't hear him. She removed her headphones and tapped her desk again until he risked another look. When he raised his head, Adrianna waved enthusiastically, but he only looked around a moment and dropped his head again. Was he just ignoring her now? What a butthole!

She took out a honey candy from her pocket, unwrapped it, popped the candy in her mouth, and rolled the wrapper into a ball. When she tapped the desk again, and he again looked up at her, she threw the wrapper at him to get his attention. Unfortunately, that didn't give the response she was hoping for. The wrapper hit him square in the face, causing him to jump in his seat, jerk his head around the room, and stare back down at black dot covered pages covering his desk. What the heck? What was wrong with him? She was right in front of him. How could he not have seen that coming? Was he blind or some... Oh God!

The rest of that day did not end as abruptly as she would have liked. The last two hours of school seemed to go on for an eternity. All she could think about was shutting herself in her room, probably for at least the next twenty years. Maybe she could run away and join a cult. A cult with a healthcare and dental plan. Anything to avoid being known at school as the girl who bullied the blind kid on his first day. There goes any chance of the boy in sunglasses ever wanting to talk to her.

The entire bus ride home, Adrianna did as much research as she could on how people who are blind go about their daily lives. She was determined to find some way to connect with him and make things right. An image she found reminded her of the black dots covering the paper on his desk. They seemed to make some type of pattern. Of course, it was Braille. That's it. Thanks *Wikipedia*. All she had to do was learn Braille. Then she could write him an apology note, all would be forgiven, and they would get married and grow old together on an Alpaca farm in Massachusetts. It was a perfect plan.

She felt that she must contact with Tom Cruise to help him planning in the next Mission Impossible sequels.

Right after dinner, she shut herself in her room and went to work writing the note. Using a Braille alphabet chart that she found online, she began to draw little black dots into blank sheets of paper, mimicking the letter patterns to create complete sentences along the page. Minutes turned to hours, as page after page began to fill with the dotted patterns. Realizing that it was nearly three in morning, Adrianna decided that the 16-page life story she had created would have to be good enough. She satisfyingly passed out on her bedroom desk.

Tomorrow shot to life at the sound of Adrianna's mom pounding on her bedroom door, warning her that bus would be at the driveway any minute. Mornings like this made Adrianna wish that she was old enough to like coffee, but today was far too important to be tired. She crammed her Braille biography into her backpack, popped a honey candy, and hurried outside, ecstatic for the day ahead.

She figured she would give the note to the boy in sunglasses in study hall. There were far too many witnesses in geography class, which could make him, feel nervous about reading it. The anticipation made morning classes drag on. The uneasy morning intensified in third period Algebra as she realized that she forgot to do the homework last night. But, as they say, "C's get degrees." Also, she had her future ahead of her; she couldn't waste her time on trivial things like Algebra.

Lunch soon came and went. Today was chicken nuggets. They were just okay. Sometimes they way more spicy than required for humans.

Finally, it was study hall. She had her headphones in, but no music was playing. The stack of paper was shaking in her hands. She took chance glances behind her to make sure he was still there. Every time, she saw him reading the little black dots covering the pages of a book, moving his hand across the page.

With sudden impulse, she shot out of her desk, took a step towards him, and plopped the pages on his desk. He gasped, "Dah, Jesus! Uh... hey. What's up?" He slid the stack towards himself, placing his hand on the top page. "Oh, uh...yea this is great...uh...thanks." He slide her note to the corner of his desk.

She didn't get it. Did he not want to read it? Did she do it wrong? The sentences she wrote looked just like what was in his book. The letters on the book just stuck out of the page a bit more... Crap.

Still looking embarrassed, the boy in sunglasses remarked, "You know, I don't have like Spidery sense or anything. So I can't tell if you're still there or not. So...I'm just gonna assume you left. So...uh...okay cool."

She understood now what she had to do. She darted back towards her desk, grabbed her books, and fled Mr. S's room.

Shortly after leaving the room, she realized there was still 45 minutes of study hall left. Adrianna returned to her desk, and sat quietly the rest of class. But once the rest of the school day was over, she knew what she had to do.

As soon as she got home that night, she snatched a bag of chocolate chips from the kitchen cupboard. They were pretty old chocolate chips so she figured they wouldn't be missed. The bag was also almost empty, but she only needed five of them to get her message across.

Bringing the bag of chocolates into her room, and finding a bottle of glue hidden in her desk, she began work on the second draft of her note. She couldn't help but recite the almost-jingle that elementary school had drilled into her head, "a little bit of glue does a lot," as she glued the chocolate chips onto a blank piece of paper to make a new pattern.

It was perfect. Now the boy in sunglasses could feel the bumps on the page from the chocolate chips and be able to read her message. She passed out after two minutes of admiring her work.

Tomorrow came just as unwelcomed as the day before. The extra couple hours of sleep didn't help at all. Doctors don't know what they're talking about. Adrianna forced herself to her feet and tossed the note into her lunch bag. Her lunch bag was insulated so it would keep the chocolate chips from melting in her locker. Today's lunch was hamburgers, so it was the perfect day to bring a lunch. Pretty sure the hamburgers were made of rubber. One time, a kid's burger fell off of their tray, hit the floor, and nearly bounced back onto his tray. At least, that was the rumour. Tomorrow was mini corn dogs, which was a completely different story. Mini corn dogs were great.

Morning classes once again took their sweet time in her anticipation to see the boy in sunglasses. After lunch, she was able to scan over her note one last time before going into study hall. Today, she couldn't even sit at her desk. She stood against the wall near where he usually sat, rapidly tapping her foot, clutching onto the note. When he entered the room, she just barely missed kicking his walking stick racing over to his desk.

She waited for him to get settled in and get his books out. She raced over and let the note fall onto his hands, making sure to be a little gentler this time. "What's this?" he asked, sliding his hand across the page. "Is this...are these chocolate chips?" She giggled silently. "Why are they stuck...are they glued? What kind of foolishness... Wait...is this? Is this supposed to be Braille?"

Adrianna wore a proud grin as he began to piece it all together. "I mean," he continued, "Surely they're supposed to be closer together."

Damn.

"But, it has to be." Moving his hand over the chocolate chips again, "H...hi? Oh...hi!" He smiled up at her.

She felt her face growing red, as she pushed back a lock of her hair behind her ear. Nailed it!.

"Do you...do you know Braille? Where did you learn Braille? What's your name?"

Uh oh. Adrianna froze in place. She didn't think she'd get this far. How was she going to answer him? How could she have possibly thought that she'd be able to have a conversation with him? It seemed the entire room was bearing down on her. Her smile faded as she turned around and sank into her desk.

His cautious voice came from behind her. "My name's Jeffrey, by the way." She bit her bottom lip, trying to keep a grin from covering her face. Today was a win.

That night, Adrianna had a new plan. She asked her dad to take her to the grocery store to get more chocolate chips. After dinner, she locked herself in her room and went to work gluing more chocolate chips on a large piece of paper. She could create patterns with the chips and write underneath the pattern what letter it represented. After a few hours of gluing chocolate to paper (a little bit of glue does a lot), she had her own Braille alphabet chart. This would be perfect. Now she could tell Jeffrey anything she wanted. Satisfied and ready for tomorrow, Adrianna went to bed.

After a seemingly endless night, tomorrow arrived. She figured she may have gotten a solid three hours of sleep last night. But that didn't matter. The excitement of the day made her feel more awake than she'd been all week. Carefully placing the chocolate chip alphabet into her backpack, she proceeded to get ready for school. Since it was mini corn dogs today, she didn't need to pack a lunch, which greatly reduced her morning routine.

Geography was the same as usual, starting with a few morning announcements from Mrs. Aniston-Bell. She couldn't stop looking towards the front row where Jeffrey sat. She couldn't wait to show him the alphabet chart she made. And at the sound of mini corn dogs, she couldn't wait for lunch either. It was nice not to have to worry about making a lunch this morning. Her lunch bag did good work holding onto her note yesterday though. Without it, it was a sure thing that the chocolate chips would have melted in her sauna of a locker

"Wait.....Ohhh.....N-Noo..."

After an aching 50 minutes of geography class, she bolted out of the classroom. Two or three books may have slipped out of her arms on the race through the hallway, but she could get those later.

Arriving at her locker, she swung open the door and dove into her backpack. Her heart sank. Pulling the now ugly, brown-smeared piece of paper out of her locker, she held back tears. A silent, defeated scream overcame her.

She stuffed the note into her pocket, popped a couple honey candies, and gathered up the rest of her fallen things, as she paced down the hall. There was still one person she knew that could help.

Entering a classroom full of desktop computers, Adrianna made her way to the back of the room, where a stocky, elderly woman sat. Students were still filing in, so their class hadn't begun yet.

"Hello, dear," the woman exclaimed with a genuine smile on her weathered face. "And to what do I owe this pleasure?" Ms. Parkinson was delightful. Adrianna loved having her as a teacher last year, even if she believed that a whole class devoted to typing on a computer was a waste of time. Ms. Parkinson's figure most closely resembled the features of a pumpkin: perfectly round with a little gray top. Adrianna guessed that she had to be at least 100 years old. Or maybe like 55. That's not even near LOL!

Slamming her books onto Ms. Parkinson's desk, Adrianna placed a closed right fist, thumb sticking up, over her left hand and moved her hands back and forth, towards Ms. Parkinson and then towards herself.

"What is it, dear? What do you need help with?"

She pulled the ruined alphabet chart out of her pocket, thrusting it into Ms. Parkinson's hands. "And what do we have here?"

Ms. Parkinson pulled on her reading glasses from their resting place around her neck. "Please tell me you didn't find this in the bathroom again, Adrianna." Ms. Parkinson looked over her glasses at Adrianna, with a slight smirk.

Adrianna returned the look with an unflinching stare.

"Okay. Okay. Only teasing, dear!"

Ms. Parkinson studied the chart for a few more seconds. Then she lowered the piece of paper, took off her glasses, and beamed at Adrianna. "Oh deary, don't you worry about a thing. I'll go see Jessica right after class, and we'll see if she can't help us out."

Adrianna didn't know who Julie was, but Ms. Parkinson's comforting look gave her a feeling of relief. She smiled back at Ms. Parkinson as the bell rang. "Now, if you don't mind, dear. I do have a class to teach. And, if I'm not mistaken, you may have one that you need to be getting off to yourself, hmm?"

Morning classes continued more smoothly, though many of her teachers were beginning to get upset by her lack of finished homework lately. Once lunch time came, her nerves really sank in. What if Ms. Parkinson wasn't able to get help before study hall? How would she be able to talk to Jeffrey then? She could barely stomach one of her mini corn dogs. The majority of her lunch break was spent staring at them, rolling them back and forth inside of her to-go box. She never disliked mini corn dogs as much as she did in that moment. Stupid, delicious bastards!

Calling lunch early, she slumped her way over to study hall. She made sure to grab her headphones so that she could get some homework done. She decided to get into Mr. S's room early so that Jeffrey wouldn't hear her walk in, and she could pretend to be invisible for the rest of the day. As she approached the open door of the classroom, a delighted voice came from behind her, "Oh, Adrianna, deary. I'm glad I caught you."

Adrianna jerked around, nearly spilling the heap of books in her hands. Her mouth flung open in delight to see the little pumpkin-shaped woman waddling toward her. "I spoke to Jessica," Ms. Parkinson continued. "And she was kind enough to lend us one of her own keys for us to use. I hope this is what you're looking for." Ms. Parkinson handed Adrianna a thick sheet of paper that looked exactly the same as the alphabet chart that she made. Though, instead of chocolate ships, the patterns above the letters were just little bumps in the page. It was so professional looking.

She couldn't believe it. Ms. Parkinson did it. Ms. Parkinson saved her. Adrianna couldn't stop herself from throwing her arms around Ms. Park's neck.

"Heh heh heh. Oh no worries, now deary. Glad I could help," she gasped.

Adrianna released Ms. Park, and the old woman smiled, gave her a wink, and waddled herself back down the hallway. Some heroes don't wear capes. Some heroes waddle...and are shaped like pumpkins.

Beaming at the new alphabet chart, Adrianna found a reborn purpose and excitement. Also, now she was hungry. She wished she hung onto a few of those mini corn dogs. She popped a few more honey candies, just to have something to eat.

The next couple minutes brought the rest of the students to fill into the classroom, including Jeffrey. As soon as he sat down, she shot out from her desk and slammed the alphabet in front of him. "Sweet Jesus!" he spat. "Give me a heart attack?" Taking notice of the large sheet of paper in front of him, "So what's all this then? Oh, moved on from chocolate chips then have we?"

Adrianna was taken aback. He continued, "Probably wondering how I knew it was you. You see, with my condition, I have certain heightened abilities. For example, I can smell fear." A drawn-out, awkward silence filled the room. He quickly added, "I'm kidding. That...that was a joke. Uh...I did, though, catch your perfume. Little stronger today. I mean, I'm not saying that's a bad thing. It's really nice, actually."

She blushed as another lock of hair found its way behind her ear.

"But uh...so that's enough out of me, heh. Uh...why don't you tell me something about you? I never got your name. Unless you want me to just call you Toto." Before she could think of any reaction, he went on, "Yea, I know it's been you this whole time. You may not be as distinct as you think you."

Adrianna was not expecting this level of sass. Was he just being cautious before, because he wasn't sure if he was talking to anyone? Maybe he was starting to get comfortable with her. Whatever it was, she couldn't back down now. She had to make her move.

"So, uh...what's up, Toto? How's the uh...how's the weather...oh cold hands!" She reached out and grabbed his right hand. It felt very warm. She guided his hand to the top of the alphabet chart. "A? A what?" She continued moving his hand along the page, stopping and touching the remaining letters ' d-r-i-a-n-n-a (picking his hand up over the 'n' and setting it back down on the same spot)-a'. "Adrianna? Is that your name?" She started shaking his hand joyously. There was an odd, warm feeling in hearing him say it.

"But, heh, why couldn't you just tell me that?"

She moved his hand to spell out more letters: 'i-c-a-n-t-s-p-e-a-k'.

"Oh. I'm...I'm so sorry." There was another silence between them. "But, then...how do you, like, talk to people?"

Moving his hand again, she spelled: 's-i-g-n'.

"Sign? Oh, you mean like sign language? Yea, I've heard teachers talk about it at my old school. Heh, guess I never really paid much attention to it, seeing how little good it would do me."

There it was: the inescapable obstacle that stood between them. How could something that's been such a huge part of her life not even exist to him? Sure, she could learn Braille as well as she could, but not being able to even imagine sign. How could she ever feel that she could truly connect with him? How could she have been so...

"Could you teach me?", said he. Well, this wasn't how Adrianna planned her day to go, but she couldn't have hoped for better. She lifted her desk and swung it around, causing all of her books to crash to the floor in the process. She could pick those up later. Once they sat facing each other, all she could do was beam at his eager face.

After a couple seconds of that, Jeffrey said, "Well it sounds like you're still here, so I'm hoping that means a yes."

Oh right. She probably should answer him somehow. Nabbing his right hand across the desks, she closed it into a fist and shifted it up and down in a nod.

"Is that a yes?"

She did again, more enthusiastically.

"God, I hope that means yes. Otherwise, I don't think we're gonna get very far."

Adrianna took his other hand and guided it along the page again to spell out 'y-e-s' while continuing to nod his other fist.

"Awesome! So if that's 'yes', then what's 'no'?"

Hmm... 'no' was going to be a little more complicated to make his hand do without being awkward and a little confusing. Adrianna decided that instead of doing the correct sign for 'no', she could just do what her mom did when she told her 'no' as a kid.

"Ow!" The sudden smack nearly made Jeffrey jump out of his chair. Rubbing the back of his hand, he sarcastically said, "I have a feeling that's not actually what 'no' is."

She giggled again. This was gonna be fun.

"Well alright then. This uh...this should be fun." Adrianna was relieved they were on the same page and that he wasn't upset about the hand slap. "Thank you."

Grabbing his hand, she uncurled his fingers, touched the tips of them to his lips, and then slowly moved his hand away from his face.

"Oh, awesome! Well thank you." He did the motion again, but this time, touched his chin instead of his lips. "Ow!"

Maybe full words and phrases are a little much to start with. She decided that, for today, they would just go through the alphabet. Closing his fist again, moving his thumb off to the side of his hand, she placed his other hand on the 'a' on the paper. Adrianna repeated the motion a few more times until Jeffrey was able to make the 'a' on his own. Then they moved on to 'b'.

They continued this through the alphabet, stopping to occasionally give Jeffrey's hand a good smacking when he did the wrong the letter, or when he complained that 'a', 'm', 'n', 's', and 't' were all basically the same thing.

When they finished the last letter, Jeffrey remarked, "I feel like they just ran out of hand-shapes. Just kinda started waving fingers around at the end. I mean, that's just lazy writing."

She giggled to herself.

"Really hoping you're laughing at some of these. Cuz I'd like to think I'm funny, but this is honestly the best I got."

She shook his fist again, encouragingly

"Heh heh. Well thank you." He touched his fingers to his lips this time.

Adrianna grabbed his hands again, and had him spell out her name.

"Oh there's no way I'm gonna be able to remember this. I mean, doing the 'n' twice just seems wasteful. Can't you just have one?"

After multiple unsuccessful attempts at her name, Jeffrey took a stab at spelling his own name: 'j-f-e-r-r-y'. Not bad for a first try. She was pretty sure two of those letters were right, at least.

Several tries later, 'j-e-f-r-e-y' being the closest attempt, the crushing ring of the bell marked the end of their study session. Adrianna moved her desk back and began picking up her books.

Jeffrey smirked towards her. "This was fun. I'll uh...see you later...err umm talk to you later...I mean...uh...bye." He did a quick wave before turning back and hurried out of the room. Getting back upright, she pushed a lock of hair behind her ear.

She mouthed the word 'bye'.

That night, she lay in her bed restlessly. Her mind was filled with thoughts of Jeffrey, and just how perfectly today went. Jeffrey was perfect. He was cute. Hilarious. She couldn't believe that a guy like him would be interested in her. So much that he would learn sign for her.

Suddenly, a terrifying feeling overcame Adrianna. He's too perfect. Once people start to get to know him, all the girls at school will fall in love with him. He's not going to stay single for long. And that's even if he still is single. He could be married. Have three kids and a small alpaca farm of his own in Massachusetts.

Okay, maybe she was getting a bit ahead of herself. But she needed to act fast. It was now or never while they were on good terms.

Springing out of bed, she pulled the Braille alphabet out of her bag. Jeffrey must have wanted her to keep it since he left it on his desk when he left study hall. She began cutting out letters, and gluing them to a sheet of paper (a little bit of glue does a lot). Realizing her note needed to repeat letters, she bolted to the kitchen to get chocolate chips.

Getting to the cupboard with the chocolate chips, her heart sank even further. Five chocolate chips. There was only five left. How many chocolate chips does her family go through? And who leaves just five chocolate chips in the bag? The chocolate chip economy sucks these days.

She decided that, hopefully, two of them would be enough to get her message across. She ate the other three. Through a little more letter arranging and gluing, her note was complete. Adrianna spent the rest of the night staring at the note.

The night blended into tomorrow, as her alarm needlessly went off. She was already packing the note into her lunch bag. She had no idea what was for lunch today. She wasn't feeling hungry anyway. A honey candy would be sufficient sustenance.

Geography class came way too soon. She walked along the front of the classroom. Jeffrey was already in his desk. The note was out in front her, shaking uncontrollably in her hand. When she passed over his desk, her grip locked, unable to drop the note. She collapsed into her desk at the back of the class, panting. It felt like the note weighed a ton; why couldn't she let go of it?

Mrs. Aniston-Bell went on with her lecture as always, though it felt like 50 minutes of just morning announcements, as Adrianna could hardly take in a word of it. The topics she picked up on blurred from a midterm exam on Monday, to Kermit the Frog getting a colonoscopy. God, she was so tired. Hopefully, her teacher didn't notice her, eyes half-closed, staring at the back of Jeffrey's head the entire class period.

The sudden ring of the bell shot a boost of adrenaline into Adrianna. Note in hand, she bustled to the front of the class, slipped it into Jeffrey's hand as he was putting a book away, and darted out of the room.

Realizing she forgot all of her stuff, she jogged back in a few seconds later. Jeffrey was still in his desk, looking around the room nervously, tucking the note into his pocket. By the time the classroom had cleared enough so that she could get her stuff, Jeffrey was long gone.

The rest of her morning classes painfully chugged along. Most of them included a personal lecture from her teacher on why she hadn't finished any of her homework this week. She grudgingly apologized, just wanting to get this day over with. At least with this whole Jeffrey mess over with, she'd be able to get back to getting homework done.

Lunch was Italian dunkers. Whoever decided to put cheese on old sub sandwich bread and call it a meal was obviously not a dietitian! She only brought the note in her lunch bag, so she figured she'd at least try to eat some of the school lunch. Unfortunately, Italian dunkers were still one of the best foods that the cafeteria served. Adrianna would usually eat them, but today she could only stare at them, playing with the questionably edible cheese. Even the thought of just having a honey candy made her want to throw up.

She walked into study hall nearly five minutes late. Mr. S, of course, didn't notice. She sat in her desk in front of Jeffrey; he didn't say anything. Did he even bother to read the note? Of course he did. That's why he looked so embarrassed and tried to hide it. Maybe he didn't want anybody to see that some loser had a crush on him.

But...no one else could read it, could they? Maybe he just didn't know who it was from. She didn't have enough chocolate chips to put her name on it. But...who else could it have been from? Surely, there would be hundreds of girls willing to learn Braille for him.

Did the hour they spent together mean nothing to him? He probably doesn't remember a single sign that she taught him. Of course he didn't. It's not like he liked her or anything. Why would he? How could she have been so stupid? She buried her head into her hands. Even if he couldn't see it, she refused to let him hear her cry.

Suddenly, a subtle tapping noise came from behind her. It had a familiar rhythm to it. It couldn't be...

She spun around in her seat. He was looking up at her. He didn't say anything. He raised his right hand in a fist, thumb to the side. He continued to spell out the rest of her name perfectly, even remembering to do the 'n' twice.

The two beamed at each other. He raised his fist again, extending his pinky. He continued to spell out: 'i-l-i-k-e-y-o-u-t-o-o'.

V

The Bashful Kid

Risav woke up when the alarm clock rang loudly with a harsh tone imitating the crying of a Hen generally seen in the bourgs. It was 7 a.m. in the morning. Risav Mukherjee, probably one of the most unwanted members of his family full of brains. Do not take this phrase on brains sarcastically. His family members have literally got brains. His father works in a multinational company and earns in lacs. He is an alumnus from the business school of Columbia University in USA. In case you haven't heard that, just 'Google' it. It's the easiest way to collect information nowadays but that hardly lasts for some days in our brains. And now people have given up reading books. His mother is a professor. We all can expect danger when mothers are teachers or professors or some sort of educational personality. Mothers without a degree in education are lot more dangerous that the Southside Serpents and Ghoulies as shown in Riverdale web series. Watch that in case you were too busy writing exams this year 'online'. Well mothers are always dangerous in terms of teaching and 'Mother Teacher' plays an irreplaceable part in our life. So do not take any offence because both Risav and I love our mothers. Let's be back to the text. I'm being a jerk rather that narrating a story.

Whatever maybe, Risav is not a good boy in terms of marks obtained in academics. Here academics is exams obviously. Exam is what the students experience their school life the most. Though Risav reads in 9th Standard, on seeing his physical appearances, it seems that he is not fit for his class. He has got a not-at-all-impressing body structure. He's tall, skinny boy with a round head, slightly pointed nose, big hairs which fall down the eyes even after combing. Though he is not a good marks gainer, traces of creativity are found in him.

Once there was a small debate-like class held by their English teacher Mr. Bose. He asked the students to reflects their views on 'Elizabeth Bennet' from the Pride & Prejudice. And hence, feminism clicked. A girl raised her hand.

Mr. Bose always spoke in a poetic voice. He said, "Here's Anusha to say about Elizabeth Bennet, please speak!"

She started, "Elizabeth Bennet was one of the best feminist revolutionary character. She dared to reject Darcy, an influential man with all powers and recommendations, thousands of likes and proposals around him."

Mr. Bose said, "Well Anusha now let's hear from some boy and you please wait until one speaks. Your words very powerful no doubt."

Anusha, being too much praised, tried bowing (that happens when you watch too much of classic movies) in honour but sir had already turned to find someone else to speak.

Sir said, "Well I need someone from boys to speak. Mmmm..Jeet please speak up!"

A boy stood. He was like the smartest boy in the class who could crack jokes at any moment and would perform in class as a topper. But everything is not what it seems from a distance. One who observes Jeet nearly could say that he pretended to be smart but the actual smart, witty and matured ones are often ignored.

Sir said, "Jeet, do you know the writer of the novel we are talking about?"

Jeet looked around in a hope that someone would at least prompt him the answers but his friends were also the same, 'the pretending ones'.

Jeet said in a low voice, "I...I think it..is....Shakespeare maybe." The girls burst out laughing aloud. Well, they were again impressed with his stupidity like they always are.

Sir said, "Jeet, it's better you sit down."

"Anybody else?", Mr. Bose asked.

Suddenly Risav raised his hand and everyone was in shock!

Mr. Bose said, "O-Okay.....any other boy except Risav who has something to say?"

Most of the boys were quiet because they generally studied the night before the exams and passed. 'Pride and Prejudice' was not just out-of-the-box but very out-of-the-box content.

Mr. Bose said, "Okay Risav, your views please!"

"Sir I feel that Elizabeth Bennet was way more arrogant than anyone else. She was attracted to Darcy and his luxurious life of high society but denied due to arrogance!"

Anusha rose with a bang. She was a topper after all. She said, "Nonsense! She was never attracted to Darcy. Darcy proposed her, got rejected and himself came back to be finally accepted by her."

Risav continued calmly," I feel you must read the novel again. You are just simply out of the actual context. If Darcy was arrogant and Elizabeth not in love, then why did she accept her?"

"We're not here to discuss their love. I want to say that she had self-respect while Darcy had to abandon his self-respect for her."

"Well, no one loses or gains self-respect in love. That means Ah..hh...Okay!..."

As Risav fumbled, Mr. Bose said, "Risav! Something more you want to say and conclude?"

"Yes sir"

"Then please continue"

Risav said, "Sir as Anusha said that Darcy abandoned his self-respect, it means that Elizabeth indirectly or directly and forcefully ripped off his dignity and pride which is a kind of humiliation!"

Every boy had smiled and some even made gestures of saluting. This one debate which hardly lasted for ten minutes just raised his respect to another level.

There was recess break after the class. When Risav was having his very usual tiffin, 'cakes and fruits', his classmates came joyously and shared their tiffin because today Risav protected their dignity by smashing the pride of Elizabeth Bennet.

Risav was very happy today. While returning from school in the bus, he generally didn't talk much with anyone. Actually, he didn't have anyone to talk. He is generally quiet and people don't poke a quiet street dog unless very excited. He just looked out of the window. The highways, people moving in cars, some in bikes, big trucks on their destination. Some days, there are accidents on the highways. He feels pity for the victims. When he looks out of the window, the world seems gliding away very fast as if it is indulged in some sort of race. He often recalls the dialogue from '3 Idiots' movie on seeing the scenario of race, "Life is a race. If you don't run faster than others, then people will smash you to go forward." Well, Risav thinks that the world has really taken this wrong concept of living to the heart which will bring consequences in the future.

As I said, Risav's house was full of brains. His father was in some office tour to London-Birmingham for about a month. But Alas! 'exam sucks', for both Risav and his mother. Risav is struggling with bundles of exams taken by his school. Reading in a modern world in so called 'English-medium school' has many disadvantages. One of them is obviously exams. The schools take more exams than the life takes. In every two months, some sort of exam, or surprise tests or some very meaningless speaking assessments would come up. And one more factor for admitting students in these sick modern world English schools of India is to make the children fluent in English. But I don't find more than hundred good English language orators among thousand students.

Now in case someone adult is reading my piece, you must be angry and thinking that the writer has no idea about student life, today's education, career struggles. Let me tell you that the narrator is a student. One of those quiet one's. Whatever, I am moving out of my story. I am an overthinker. I keep on wandering from the actual path. Life's very tough. We teenagers just like Risav swim into memes to give ourselves some temporary relief from the crowds running for that worthless, invisible trophy. Ahh.... again, I'm out of my text. Let's come back from where I left.

Risav came back to his house. There were only Risav and his parents living in his house. His father was out for tour. Risav also has two uncles (Father's Brothers), their wives and each pair having a son. All live with Risav's grandmother in Burdwan. A town in West Bengal. Risav went hardly went once or twice to his grandmother's house. His grandma is always busy in the prayer room worshipping god and spreading some baseless superstitions through her maid who comes for washing dishes and gains grandma's knowledge. And her TV serial! Risav felt going mad. The actors in the TV serials are generally hated or loved based on their performances. But Risav hated the writer of the story and also the one human who wrote those vulnerable dramatic dialogues! And also showed some stuff called Romance. Seeing those, even Shakespeare would also laugh from heaven...or hell. Because we don't know about people's sins.

As Risav started going upstairs, his mother nearly screamed from the kitchen like any other Bengali mother does. That's very normal actually.

"Risav you're back home?", she didn't bother to wait for an answer and continued, "You get freshened up, come down and eat quickly. You've got tuition at 5. It's A-L-R-E-A-D-Y 4:30 p.m., Oh my god!"

Risav took a deep breathe, trying not to protest this irritating reminder and went upstairs. He dashed into his room, slammed the door and sat in his study table. It's always messy. Full of books, papers, pens, pencils and other stuffs. He took out his very thick five-year diary. He got this as a gift from aunt two months ago. He is not a great writer though. He sometimes writes for pages and sometimes he just writes a single word or a phrase.

He opened the diary and wrote:

12/7/2018

Life is just turning into some sort of shit :(

VI

Medusa's Wrath

Benjamin sat on the chair beautifully made up of Lazarus wood in the study room, something he had often heard but saw with his eyes for the first time. It was the house of Mr.Vikram Rampaul, a renowned man. He was one of the most influential researcher on Greek mythology in India and Bangladesh.

Benjamin Mathews Raderson is a journalist, who has recently joined The New York Times and planning to write weekly articles on some unusual happenings related to Greek Mythology.

Mr.Rampaul entered the study room and sat on the chair in front of Benjamin. He took a glass from the side table and poured whiskey in it. He asked Benjamin with a twisted eyebrow,"A drink?"

Benjamin looked at his watch which indicated it was 6 in the evening and not the best timeto drink when you are there for a work.

"Uhh, no, thanks!"

"Hey come on, its already evening, have one." Mr.Rampaul started pouring whiskey in another glass and passed it to Benjamin.

"So, Mr.Randerson, I read your email, but you see its very personal. Ahmed was one of my closest friends and I cannot reveal something like this to the world. It is unethical. Atleast I feel it."

Benjamin was prepared for this. His years of experience has taught him that denial is the first step for everyone. He said,"Sir, I assure you this will be completely personal. I will make sure that the names and every other significant details that can harm your friend's privacy is changed. We mean no harm to anyone but just explore unnatural happenings. Not some boring horror stories that people listen to."

Mr.Rampaul took a deep breath and thought something for a minute. He said,"Fine, I am sharing this only with you assurance but if anything wrong happe-"

"You don't worry sir, I am taking the responsibility."

Mr.Rampaul kept the glass on the table. He stood up ad went to the old wooden cupboard. He opened it and took out an old album.

He handed it to Benjamin. Benjamin opened it. It had the pictures of Mr.Rampaul, from around 30 years ago with a person. The other man was young, nicely built and tall. His dark blue eyes showed huge depth.

Mr.Rampaul started,"I was in Bangladesh in the 90s. I got the job of professor in Greek mythology. Although I was Indian, I studied at London and therefore getting a good job in some foreign country that time was not that tough. I met Ahmed there in Dhaka. He stayed in my neighbourhood and worked in a private company at some manager post. Just like me, he was not very rich or poor. Saying that we were some sort of middle-class residents would be appropriate. We were unmarried. So we spent the evenings after work gossiping, playing cards or sometimes going to our colleague's parties which were very rare. But Ahmed was always smiling.

But slowly I started private tuitions because everyone of us wants to earn some more. I felt that the salary as a professor in a college wasn't enough. Our evening gossips started reducing because I got busy with tuitions. Ahmed also had pressure of work from office. But then one day he called me. We had telephones only at that time. I picked up the phone and was astonished hearing his voice because he hardly called me. I picked up the phone and he told me to immediately go to his house. Fortunately I did not have any tuitions that day because the students had some exam. I wore a jacket because it was January and the weather was very cold outside. He rented the ground floor of a house. The first floor was locked by the owners and they lived somewhere else.

I went to his house and ringed the bell twice. I heard heavy footsteps coming towards the door and then Ahmed opened the door. He was looking very excited, sweating even in this chilly weather, which wasn't natural for sure.

Through the narrow corridor from the front door, there were stairs on right which went upper floors and on the left was another wooden door opening to a small living room. Through the living room which looked very empty due to almost no such furniture, we entered Ahmed's bedroom.

Ahmed said, "I had always remained busy with work and hardly looked in details of this house. It's a rental house after all. But yesterday while cleaning, I noticed this alcove covered with the brown coloured cloth. As I touched the alcove, I felt like it's something like a door. I opened it but nothing was visible inside. So, I called you, hoping that we could explore it together.

He pointed at the alcove and as I was going near it, the electricity cut off. This was a very severe problem those days. Ahmed found one torch and a candle. I lighted the candle and holding it on a candle stand, started going inside the alcove. Ahmed was at the front, with his torch. The space was so less that we almost had to sit and move. After moving for around two minutes, it opened to a big room. At the first sight we were terrified, because there was a snakeskin on the floor. It was winter, so there were less chances of a snake to be there, but we still checked around and suddenly Ahmed pointed towards a statue.

We looked at the statue. Around the statue were some very old plates and glasses. It was most probably worshipped long time back, either by someone who stayed as rental or the house owners. We took the statue and came back to the bedroom, covering the alcove with that brown cloth.

The electricity was back. Ahmed kept the statue on the table. We looked at it very closely, although could not recognise which goddess it was. It looked very frightening yet attractive. It was a statue of a woman holding a sword in one hand, wearing a white cloth and on the head, instead of hairs, came out snakes, curling over each other.

I said, "Ahmed, its not our property. I feel you should keep it back where it was. I cannot recognise this statue but I don't think it's something good."

I don't know if Ahmed listened to me and decided to ignore, or didn't listen actually. He pushed the statue at the corner of the table and said, "Let this statue be here. I will keep it back inside that room in the morning. I think you should go back and have some sleep. Its already very late and the temperature is going down."

I bid him good night and came back to my his that night. Wish I had stayed at his house that night!

After that I got busy with my work. Also, I went back to India for a month on death of my father. When I came back to Dhaka, I called Ahmed. But he didn't pick up my call. So, I went to his house one evening. It was around April and the temperature was quite hot. He opened the door, and I was pretty shocked looking at him. He had gained a lot weight, looked quite different. His face looked a bit paler than I had seen him some months back. I entered his house, just as I had seen it months ago. He took me to his bedroom where I saw that old weird idol still on the table. There was a small steel plate beside it.

I asked him, "You have still kept it? Are you worshipping it or something?"

"Yes, uhh, you told me to keep it back but the idol was very attractive. I didn't have much to do in the evenings, so I passed my time looking at it. It feels good. One day I felt like the idol wanted food. So, I give it food twice everybody. You can say it's kind of worshipping, but for me its like a new hobby. "

On hearing this I did not feel right because I always felt that I had seen this type of idol somewhere and whatever it depicted, it wasn't good.

I said, "But I think it is better if you don't involve with this. You don't even know what it is!"

He said, "Don't worry dear, I am not that religious kind of a person or something. If you don't mind, its my evening time with the lady idol. I like the spend this time alone."

He said this with a smile but I was struck by his words because I was his best company. It was not that I felt jealous or something, but I could feel Ahmed changing a lot.

After that a lot of things happened. Ahmed got promotions in his office. Got busier with his work and our contact started to fade quickly. He then invested in stocks and made a lot of money in quick intervals. He became famous among the high-class men, started spending time with them, parties, drinks. He turned quite indiscipline, you can say. I also heard things which were very shocking. His lust for money and girls increased at a huge rate. He was always seen with some woman everywhere. He even resigned from his job. What shocked everyone was that his quick success and money. He hardly lost any money in the stocks despite of the risks involved. Some people felt it was his brains, some were obviously jealous and many thought it was his luck. It was always very mysterious to me. One day I decided to visit him. He had become very rich, but still stayed at his old house. But not in rent anymore. He had bought that house. The owners then lived at their other house in someplace at Sylhet.

I was dumbstruck on meeting him. He had become a fat man, looked more aged that he actually was. His face had become pale, as if somebody had took out all the blood from his body.

Although he was my old friend, he had completely changed and hardly took any interest in talking with me now. So, I talked with him for about ten minutes and left his house. I don't know what I was thinking, but I took a rickshaw and went Mr. Johar Ali's house. He was a retired professor of Dhaka University. Before me, he was the Head of Department of Greek Mythology and Literature. Yes, I rose to the position of Head of Department in the university. I had a few talks with him in one seminar and I thought he could help me.

My theory was that everything that was happening with Ahmed, his sudden drastic change, quick strings of success, lust, physical appearance and health, all were somehow related to that idol which we could not recognise.

Thankfully Mr. Ali was at his house and agreed to listen to me. I shared every detail with him. He listened to me and then thought something for a long time.

He said, "I have understood what idol it is! It's the idol of Medusa and I know the house in which your friend stays. I used to go to that area for teaching one of my students. The owner of that house worshipped that idol of Medusa.

Medusa was a monster in the Ancient Greek Mythology. She was female winged monster who had venomous snakes as hair, held a sword and it was believed that whoever gazed into her eyes would turn into a stone. Many people in the ancient Greek era worshipped her and it was seen that the people who worshipped her received quick success and money but unknowingly went to a path of self-destruction. The health of those people started to fall, lust for women, hunger of money increased and finally the people would die at a young age. Their bodies would turn pale, they often became very fat, angry and their personal relations were destroyed."

I thanked Mr. Ali and quickly ran to Ahmed's house and told him everything. But he seemed to completely ignore me, he rather told me to go home and have some sleep.

After around a month, Ahmed was found dead at a bar. Doctors said that it was heart failure due to weak health and drinking. But I know that all this was due to Medusa's wrath. Everyone who worships her faces this self-destruction.

I still remember Ahmed's dead face. Completely pale and looked like a stone as if he saw Medusa while dying. Maybe he had."

Mr. Rampaul finished his story and lighted another cigarette. Benjamin sat quietly, drinking his whiskey He could imagine how fearsome it was!!

VII

Is It?

Detective Murari entered the dark, smelly interrogation room. A boy of hardly 25-26 years of age is sitting at one corner of the dark room. He was brought in this room 6hours ago, but he is still smiling. As if mocking the system.

Detective Murari, aged 46, is one of the best officers of the Lal Bazaar Detective Department. It took him 11months to catch this criminal, although this boy is too young and doesn't look like he has committed any heinous crime. But years of experience in this field has taught Murari that looks can be deceiving.

Murari pulled a chair and sat opposite to the boy. He looked at him for some time. The boy was quite tall, had scruffy black hairs.

Murari said, "Now speak up. Your name?"

"As if you don't know!", the boy said with a smile.

"I have to go through the procedures. Tell me your name."

"Sam Basu. My name."

"So, Sam, you murdered 7 girls! Do have any idea how horrific it is?"

Sam didn't reply. But that small smile in his face made Murari angry. He banged the table in front of him hardly and said, "You killed 7 girls. You tore their lips by biting them. Are you even a human?"

Sam said, "You don't have to tell me how I did my job. I also stabbed them at the end. Made sure, they die before they get a chance to live again."

"And you think that's something to be proud of?"

"You asked if I am a human. Well, I used to be human. But that me has died. I am no longer a human. "

"What do you mean?"

"What I mean isn't necessary, just finish this shit and hang me."

"I need to know why you did it. Speak up. The faster you do, the faster I go."

"Fine, I loved a girl. She made fun of me because I was poor. That's all."

"Details please. I want to know everything in details, not some movie plot."

Sam cleared his voice and said, "I was in college. I saw a girl and fell in love with her. Like many other people fall. But she made fun of me. With the help of seniors, took my ragging. Tore my books, even one boy beat me up. But I didn't complain. But this went too far. The girl told one of our professors that I teased her. I got suspended. Nobody heard me. Not the professors, not my friends, even my family ignored me. I became an outskirt at home."

"And how does that make sense? You killed these girls for what? Revenge?"

"I HAVEN'T FINISHED. FOR GOD'S SAKE, ATLEAST HEAR ME OUT ONCE!!"

Murari was shocked as Sam screamed suddenly.

Sam continued, “One day I went to that girl’s home to apologise and tell her to kindly lift her complain. But instead, she told her friends that I tried to molest her. Those rich brats. They told to the head of student union of college and then registered a complain in the police station. The police arrested me; the court didn’t even bother to hear me. I got punished with a 3years imprisonment.”

“The police didn’t hear you?”

“Yes, they did.”

“But they didn’t help you?”

“Yes, they did.”

“And you still say that nobody heard you!”

“They helped me by applying their third-degree methods on me. They helped me by killing my humanity. I am justice now. What I did was giving justice which you guys failed to give.”

“I agree that what happened to you was wrong. But you could still fight for yourselves. But you chose to kill innocents.”

“I was also innocent. But nobody cared. I don’t care about innocence anymore.”

“So, you killed these girls because they were rich, and that’s justice for you?”

“Yes.”

“How did you choose these girls?”

“After I got released from jail, I went home, but they denied to recognise me. Kicked me out. I went to that girl. She laughed on seeing me. I killed her. Then I kept following her rich friends, made plans. I realised that I had turned into a madman. But that’s what humans are after everything.”

“But this just turned you into a monster. You can never have your life back!”

"I never had."
"You could have made a new start."
"It's not that easy. Is it?"

Printed by Libri Plureos GmbH in Hamburg, Germany